The Mystery of the Haunted House

by Katie Dale and Sian James

W
FRANKLIN WATTS

Chapter 1

Sarwat loved solving mysteries.

He found his sister's lost hamster ...

and Dad's missing cookies ...

and he always found Mum's lost glasses!

"I wonder what mystery I will solve next,"

said Sarwat.

"How about the mystery of the haunted house?"

said his next door neighbour, Mr Wood.

"Did you say haunted house?"

Sarwat said excitedly.

"A house can't be haunted," said Mum. "There are no such things as ghosts."

Mr Wood frowned. "We're trying to sell our house, but every time someone comes to look round strange things happen and scare them away," he said.

"What kind of strange things?" Sarwat asked.

"Yesterday the lights suddenly went out," Mr Wood said. "And this morning there were scary noises."

"How odd," said Sarwat. "Can I come to your house tomorrow and try to solve the mystery?"

Mr Wood nodded. "Someone called Mr Grey is coming to see the house tomorrow morning. You're welcome to come then too, if it's okay with your mum?"

Mum nodded. "I'll come as well. I don't believe in ghosts."

Chapter 2

The next morning, Sarwat, Mum and Mr Grey
all went to Mr Wood's house.

"This looks like a nice house," Mr Grey said,
smiling. "I think I will like it."

"Come in and let me show you around,"
said Mr Wood.

Sarwat looked around. It certainly didn't look
like the old, dark, spooky, haunted houses from
ghost stories he had read.

This house was modern and clean, and at first,
everything seemed normal.

But then they heard a strange sound ...

"Whooooooo!"

"What was that noise?" Mr Grey asked, looking scared.

"Probably just the wind," said Sarwat.

Next they went into the kitchen.

Mr Grey looked around. "This is a nice kitchen,"

he said.

But suddenly the lights went out!

"What's happening?" Mr Grey cried.

"Maybe it's an old light bulb?" said Sarwat.

"Look!" Mr Grey cried, pointing at

the kitchen window.

There, written on the glass, were the words:

"Go away!"

"Spooky sounds, lights going off and now even

strange messages!" Mr Grey cried. "This house

is haunted!" He ran away, screaming.

"Oh no!" Mr Wood sighed.

"The house can't really be haunted,"

said Mum. "Can it?"

She didn't sound quite so sure any more.

"Don't worry, 'I'll solve this mystery," Sarwat said.

15

Sarwat hurried outside and peered at

the strange writing on the kitchen window.

It was written in mud.

He looked down at the flowerbed below

the window and spotted ...

... footprints!

"Look!" Sarwat cried. "It wasn't a ghost who wrote the message – because ghosts don't wear shoes!"

Chapter 3

"If it wasn't a ghost, it must have been a person,"

Sarwat said. "But who? Can you think of anyone

who doesn't like you, Mr Wood?"

Mr Wood shook his head. "I can't think of anyone.

I'll ask my son, Tom, if he knows of anyone."

Mr Wood called Tom downstairs.

"Can you think of anyone who doesn't like us,

Tom?" he asked.

Tom shook his head.

Sarwat frowned. This was going to be

a hard mystery to solve.

"I can't believe someone would write

a scary message on our window,"

Mr Wood sighed sadly. "We're never going to

sell this house."

Everyone frowned ...

... except Tom, who was smiling.

Sarwat was puzzled. Why was Tom happy?

Chapter 4

Then Sarwat spotted a pair of muddy trainers by the kitchen door.

"Are these your shoes, Tom?" he asked, picking one up.

"Yes, I've been playing football in the back yard all morning," Tom said.

"But your back yard is paved, not muddy,"

Sarwat said, pointing.

"Except for the flowerbeds under the window ..."

Suddenly Sarwat had an idea.

"Follow me everyone!" he cried.

Sarwat put Tom's shoe next to the footprints.

"Tom's shoe is the same size as the footprint!"

Sarwat cried. "I think Tom wrote the message."

"Tom?" Mr Wood frowned. "Is this true?"

Chapter 5

Tom looked down.

"Yes," he said quietly.

"Did you make the spooky noises and turn the lights off too?" Sarwat asked.

Tom nodded. "I wanted everyone to think the house was haunted."

Mr Wood frowned. "But why?"

"I don't want anyone to buy our house,
so I wanted to scare them away," Tom sighed.
"I don't want to move. This is my home. All my
friends live around here. I thought if no one
bought the house, we could stay."

"Oh Tom!" his dad cried, hugging him. "Why
didn't you just tell me you wanted to stay here?"
"Because you wanted to move," Tom said sadly.

"Tom, what I want most of all is for you to be happy," Mr Wood said, smiling. "So we'll stay here."

"Oh thank you, Dad!" Tom cried happily.

Sarwat smiled. He'd solved another mystery and everyone was happy.

Things to think about

1. What words best describe Sarwat's character?
2. Why does Mr Grey run away from viewing the house?
3. How does Sarwat manage to solve the mystery?
4. Why does Tom feel so anxious about moving home?
5. What do you think about the ending of the story? Can you think of a family situation with similar fears and a happy resolution?

Write it yourself

One of the themes in this story is overcoming fear. Now try to write your own story about a similar theme.

Plan your story before you begin to write it.
Start off with a story map:

- a beginning to introduce the characters and where your story is set (the setting);
- a problem which the main characters will need to fix in the story;
- an ending where the problems are resolved.

Get writing! Try to use interesting descriptions such as "suddenly the lights went out" to add action to your story and excite your reader.

Notes for parents and carers

Independent reading

This series is designed to provide an opportunity for your child to read independently, for pleasure and enjoyment. These notes are written for you to help your child make the most of this book.

About the book

Sarwat is great at solving mysteries. When strange things start happening at his next door neighbour's house, Sarwat is on the case! Is the house really haunted, or can another explanation be found?

Before reading

Ask your child why they have selected this book. Look at the title and blurb together. What do they think it will be about? Do they think they will like it?

During reading

Encourage your child to read independently. If they get stuck on a word, remind them that they can sound it out in syllable chunks. They can also read on in the sentence and think about what would make sense.

After reading

Support comprehension and help your child think about the messages in the book that go beyond the story, using the questions on the page opposite. Give your child a chance to respond to the story, asking:

- Did you enjoy the story and why?
- Who was your favourite character?
- What was your favourite part?
- What did you expect to happen at the end?

Franklin Watts
First published in Great Britain in 2020
by The Watts Publishing Group

Series Editors: Jackie Hamley and Melanie Palmer
Series Advisors: Dr Sue Bodman and Glen Franklin
Series Designers: Cathryn Gilbert and Peter Scoulding

A CIP catalogue record for this book is
available from the British Library.

ISBN 978 1 4451 7251 4 (hbk)
ISBN 978 1 4451 7256 9 (pbk)
ISBN 978 1 4451 7260 6 (library ebook)
ISBN 978 1 4451 8067 0 (ebook)

Printed in China

Franklin Watts
An imprint of
Hachette Children's Group
Part of The Watts Publishing Group
Carmelite House
50 Victoria Embankment
London EC4Y 0DZ

An Hachette UK Company
www.hachette.co.uk

www.franklinwatts.co.uk